Isla Waddlewing Breaks the Ice

Daisy Meadows

ORCHARD

Map of Friendship Forest

Can you keep a secret? I thought you could!

Then I'll tell you about an enchanted wood.

It lies through the door in the old oak tree,

Let's go there now - just follow me!

We'll find adventure that never ends,

And meet the Magic Animal Friends!

Love,
Goldie the Cat

Story One
Snow Magic

CHAPTER ONE

Sunshine Meadow

"Finished!" said Lily Hart, brushing snow from her gloves.

Lily's best friend, Jess Forester, admired their snowman. "I think he's the best we've ever made!"

Jess was right. The snowman, made of three big balls of tightly packed snow,

 9

stood almost as tall as the girls. They couldn't stop grinning, though their fingers and toes tingled with cold.

Snow lay like a soft white blanket all around them, and the garden of the Helping Paw Wildlife Hospital was peaceful and silent. Lily's parents had brought the animals into the barn, where it was cosy and warm.

"Now for the finishing touches," said Jess. She added a row of little pebbles to the snowman's face, to make a smile. Then Lily found two bigger pebbles for the eyes.

"There's just one thing missing ..." said

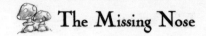

Lily, thoughtfully.

"A nose," said both girls at once. They looked at each other and laughed.

"What shall we use?" said Jess.

"I bet we can find something in the garden," said Lily. "Let's have a look."

The girls set off, boots sinking deep in the snow as they explored the garden.

"I can't see a thing but white!" said Jess. "Except – what's that?"

She pointed to a flash of gold beneath a snow-laden bush.

"It's Goldie!" said Jess.

Sure enough, a golden cat strolled out from among the leaves, and shook snow from her fur.

The girls' old friend waved her tail in the air, and let out a soft miaow.

"Are we going back to Friendship Forest?" asked Jess eagerly. Friendship Forest was a magical secret world where all the animals could talk and lived in adorable little cottages. Their friend Goldie had taken them on many adventures there.

As if in reply, Goldie set off, leaping through the snow and leaving neat little pawprints behind her. She ran to the little stream at the bottom of the garden, darted across its frozen surface and waited

on the other side, in Brightley Meadow.

"Come on!" said Lily, and the girls ran
after Goldie.

The cat led them through the
meadow to an old, dead oak tree.
As they approached, the tree burst
suddenly into life. Ivy sprouted from the
ground, winding up the ancient trunk.
The branches sparkled with frost, and
snowflakes began to fall softly all around,
like white confetti. A little robin perched
on a bough, singing sweetly.

Goldie touched her paw to the trunk,
and swirling letters appeared, carved in

the wood. Lily took Jess's hand, and the girls read the words out loud together.

"Friendship Forest!"

A little door began to form in the trunk, just big enough for the girls to fit through, with a handle shaped like an oak leaf.

Jess opened the door and a bright, golden light spilled out. After the cat darted through, the girls stepped in after their friend.

Lily and Jess closed their eyes. A tingle crept across their skin, and they knew that they were shrinking, just a little.

When they opened their eyes again the light had faded away, and they were standing among the tall, green trees of Friendship Forest.

Lily felt a droplet of water run down her face, and she realised that the snowflakes caught in their hair were melting. Sunshine fell on the forest floor, throwing leafy shadows into the little clearing.

Jess grinned. "I can't believe how warm it is here, when it's snowing at home!"

"It's magical," agreed Lily.

"Of course it is, girls," said Goldie. "It's

Friendship Forest! Welcome back."

The cat was standing on her hind legs and wore a sparkly scarf wrapped around her neck. Here in the forest, she was almost as tall as the girls.

Lily and Jess gave Goldie a big hug. "It's good to be back," said Lily. Then she frowned. "But I hope Grizelda isn't causing trouble again."

 17

Jess shivered at the mention of the horrible witch. Grizelda kept trying to drive the animals out of the forest so that she could have it all to herself. Together, the girls and Goldie had always managed to put a stop to her evil plans, but Grizelda never gave up.

Goldie just smiled and shook her head. "No one has seen her in ages," she said. "Actually, I've got a nice surprise for you. How would you like to see an ice show?"

CHAPTER TWO

Grizelda Spells Trouble

"An ice show sounds magical!" said Jess.
"We'd love to come."

"I can't wait," added Lily. "But it's so
warm and sunny here! Don't you need
ice for an ice show?"

Goldie giggled, her green eyes
sparkling. "Of course you do! But the Ice

19

Show isn't going to be in the forest. It's in Snowdrop Slopes, which is cold and snowy all year round. It's a long way north of Friendship Forest, so we'll have to take the Friendship Forest Express."

"I like the sound of that!" said Lil, grinning at Jess. The girls both knew that time stood still in their world while they were in Friendship Forest, so they could stay as long as they liked.

Goldie led the way through the forest. Birds twittered in the trees and a gentle breeze swayed the branches. Up ahead, they could hear the gentle babble of

Willowtree River. But then the babbling
noise turned into more of a strange
bubbling noise. Lily and Jess glanced at
each other.

"What is that noise?" Jess asked. "It
sounds like a kettle boiling."

"I don't know," said Goldie, "Nobody
lives near this stretch of the river – unless
the Featherbills—"

She was interrupted by a horrible
cackle ringing out through the forest. The
girls and Goldie froze.

"Uh-oh," whispered Lily. "Could that
sound be ..."

"Grizelda!" said Jess and Lily at the
same time.

Goldie's eyes went wide, and her fur
stood on end. "We'd better investigate."

The girls ran through the trees, followed
by Goldie, until they stumbled out on to
the riverbank. Jess skidded to a halt and
Lily gasped.

A woman stood by the river, hunched over a big black cauldron. She wore a glittering purple tunic and a long black cloak, and her tangled green hair hung over her face as she peered into the cauldron. The girls couldn't see what was inside, but green sparks shot out of it and fizzled on the grass, giving off a horrible

smell of rotten eggs.

"It's Grizelda," whispered Goldie, her voice quaking. "And she's casting a spell!"

"We must stop her," said Lily, bravely stepping forward.

Grizelda glanced up, and her mouth twisted into a cruel smile. "Hello there, silly girls," she crowed. "And of course, that wretched cat's here too ... Well, you've come too late to meddle. My spell is complete!"

The witch clapped her hands, and a cloud of green smoke spilled from the cauldron, spreading out in all directions. Goldie and the girls closed their eyes and coughed as the smoke surrounded them. Jess shuddered. The smoke was freezing cold!

When the girls opened their eyes again, the smoke had cleared, but everything looked different. The green grass of the riverbank was covered in a thick layer of snow. Willowtree River was a solid slick of ice, and the trees of the forest were glazed with frost.

"What have you done?" Lily demanded.

As she spoke, the clear, sunny

sky turned grey, and a chilly wind swept through the trees. Snowflakes began to fall in gusts, and the girls' teeth chattered with cold.

"I've buried the forest in ice and snow, of course!" sneered Grizelda. "Now all the animals will be so cold and miserable that they'll have to leave. Friendship Forest will finally be mine!"

The witch threw back her head and screeched with laughter. Then with a *BANG* and a shower of smelly green sparks, she was gone.

CHAPTER THREE

An Ice-Skating Penguin

The snow fell thicker and thicker, and the girls had to pull their coats back on and button them up.

"That horrible witch!" said Jess. "We can't let her get away with this."

"But what can we do?" Lily wondered.

Before the others could reply, a little

figure came zigzagging
around a bend in the
river. "It's a penguin
chick!" Jess said.
"And I think
she's wearing ice
skates!"

"And earmuffs!" said Lily.

"Why, it's little Isla Waddlewing!"
said Goldie. "But what's she doing here?
She must have skated all the way from
Snowdrop Slopes."

Isla jumped and twirled in mid-air, then
slid to a halt in a big spray of ice.

"I've never seen such a good ice-skater!" said Lily, impressed.

"Hello, Isla!" called Goldie. "These are my friends Lily and Jess."

The penguin waved a fluffy little wing. "Hello, Goldie!" she said, blinking her shiny black eyes. "And hello, girls! I'm so glad I found you. I need your help!"

"What's the matter?" asked Jess.

Isla Waddlewing hopped on to the bank.

"It's the Ice Show," she said breathlessly. "I'm supposed to be performing in it tonight, but something very strange

has happened. All the ice and snow has
disappeared!"

The girls exchanged a look – they
could both guess what had happened.
"Grizelda must have made it disappear,"
Lily explained.

"She's cast a spell to cover Friendship
Forest in snow," said Jess, "and she must
have got it all from Snowdrop Slopes."

Isla hung her little head. "That's
terrible," she said sadly. "If we don't get
our nice cold weather back, it's not just
the Ice Show that will be ruined ... None
of the animals who live in Snowdrop

Slopes will be able to stay there."

"And with all the freezing snow in Friendship Forest, the animals here won't be able to stay either," said Goldie. "What are we going to do?"

"We'll fix this," said Jess. "Won't we, Lily?"

Lily nodded, then frowned in thought. "Perhaps we should find someone who knows about snow magic."

"Mr Redbreast," said Isla. "He knows everything there is to know about snow! He lives here in Friendship Forest but often flies up to Snowdrop Slopes."

"Good idea!" said Goldie. "Let's pay him a visit."

"What about Isla?" said Jess, pointing at the penguin's skates. "She can't ice-skate through the snow."

Isla bent down and tapped her skates with a wing and said:

"*Through sparkling snow,*

Walking we go!"

At once the skates glowed an icy blue, and with a *ZZZAP!* and a sparkle of blue magic, they turned into sturdy boots.

"That's amazing!" said Lily.

"They're my special Snow Boots," Isla

said. "They can turn into anything I need.
Skates, skis, a snowboard ... You name it."
She beamed proudly. "Now let's go!"

Isla and the
girls followed
Goldie along the
riverbank. The
snow fell silently
all around, and
their footsteps
made deep prints
as they walked.

Lily felt sad to see the forest so quiet and
empty. Even the Toadstool Café had a

little CLOSED sign hung on the door. A family of squirrels were shovelling snow from outside their doorway, but more was falling all the time.

"I hope Mr Redbreast lives close by," said Jess, shivering. "It's freezing!"

"Not far now," called Goldie. She headed deeper into the forest.

Soon they came to a glade of tall fir trees, where the pine needles shone as

though they were made of silver. The

branches were hung with decorations.

There were sparkly red baubles, glittering

snow globes and twinkling fairy lights.

"They look like Christmas trees!" said

Lily.

"Magical ones," Jess agreed.

"Mr Redbreast told me all about these

beautiful trees," said Isla, her big eyes

open wide. "But I've never seen them in

real life before!"

"Welcome to Hollyberry Glade," said Goldie. "It always feels like Christmas here, thanks to Mr Redbreast! It's his favourite time of year. Look how neatly he's hung everything on the trees – he's a very tidy sort of bird."

Lily saw something moving inside one of the magical snow globes. It was a miniature mechanical mouse, ice-skating in little circles on a frozen pond. She found another globe, and saw a robin the size of a thimble, fluttering its tiny wings.

"Amazing," Lily breathed.

"Where is Mr Redbreast?" asked Jess.

Goldie pointed ahead to a tree trunk, and the girls saw a bird-sized front door there, set between the lower branches. It was painted red with a tiny holly wreath hanging on it.

"I can't see!" said Isla, hopping up and down. Jess swept the little penguin on to her shoulders.

Lily knocked gently on the

 37

door, and it swung open. Inside was a cosy little living room, but it was a terrible mess. Books and broken ornaments lay all over the floor, and pictures hung at funny angles.

"Hello?" said Lily. "Is anyone home?"

A fire crackled in the hearth, but no one answered.

"Goldie, I thought you said Mr Redbreast was tidy?" said Jess.

"He is!" Goldie said with a frown.

"Oh dear," said Isla, flapping her wings anxiously. "This isn't like Mr Redbreast at all ... I think he must be in trouble!"

CHAPTER FOUR

Shrunk!

The friends searched the glade, but there was no sign of Mr Redbreast anywhere.

"What are those?" said Jess, pointing at something in the snow.

Lily peered closer. A strange trail of prints led away from Mr Redbreast's home, disappearing in among the trees.

Each print was as big and round as a dustbin lid.

"Some giant monster must have kidnapped Mr Redbreast!" cried Isla. Tears filled her eyes, and she wiped them away with her wings.

"Let's follow the prints and see if we can find him," said Lily.

"Good idea!" said Isla, jumping off Jess's shoulders and landing in a puff of snow. They followed the tracks through the woodland, deeper and deeper into Friendship Forest. The snow was almost up to their knees now, and still falling. It

gathered in big white waves around the
trunks of the trees. Here and there, the
girls saw little houses half buried by snow,
and the worried faces of their woodland
friends peering out through the frosty
windows.

Molly Twinkletail the mouse waved
from her garden, where she and her
family were gathering firewood. "Where

 41

did all this snow come from?" she asked.

"It's that horrible Grizelda," said Jess.

"Oh dear," said Mrs Twinkletail,
shivering. "If the snow doesn't go away,
we'll have to leave Friendship Forest!"

"We'll put a stop to it," said Goldie.
"We promise!"

They hurried on. Soon the trail of
strange marks led into a darker part
of the forest, where the trees grew
close together and the branches hung
low. Voices came from behind a big
snowy bush up ahead. "Perhaps it's Mr
Redbreast," said Jess.

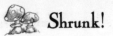

"Or his kidnappers," whispered Lily.

They darted around the side of the bush.

But there was no one there. Instead, the trail came to a halt beside a little group of snowmen, facing away from them. Each was made out of three large balls of snow with sticks for arms. One of the snowmen had a woolly hat on, while another wore a long scarf, and the third had a pointy carrot for a nose.

"What a strange place to build snowmen!" said Isla.

Lily stepped around to the front of

the snowmen. The carrot nose was
drooping slightly, so she reached out and
straightened it.

"Oi!" shouted the snowman.

Lily and Jess almost fell over with shock
as the snowman tilted his head. He glared
at them with eyes made out of coal.

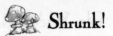

"Well?" fumed the snowman. "What do you have to say for yourself?"

"Touching strangers' noses, indeed ..." added the snowman in the hat.

"How rude!" the snowman with the scarf chipped in.

"Goodness me," said Lily. "You can talk!"

"Of course we can!" snapped the first snowman. "Why wouldn't we? We are the Enchanted Snowmen. I'm Freezy, and this is Blizzard. And that's Buttons," he said, pointing to the one with the long scarf.

"Excuse me," said Jess, "but we're

looking for a robin called Mr Redbreast."

"Have you seen him?" asked Isla.

The snowmen burst out laughing. They weren't very nice laughs.

"Of course we have," said Blizzard. "We kidnapped him!"

The friends gasped.

"Tell us where he is," said Goldie bravely.

"Hidden," said Blizzard. "Grizelda told us to hide him from you. You'll never find him, that's for sure!

"Speaking of Grizelda," said Buttons, "here's a little present from her ..."

The snowman
lifted one of his stick
arms, and an icy bolt of blue
magic shot out.

"Duck!" yelled Jess.

The friends flung
themselves to the ground. Lily and Jess
looked up just in time to see the bolt of
magic hit a tree behind them with a hiss
and a sizzle. The tree glowed blue, then it
shrank, getting smaller and smaller until it
was tiny enough to fit into the palm of a
hand.

"Next time, we'll shrink all of you!"

called Freezy. "Just like we did to your friend!"

The snowmen slid away, cackling horribly, and disappeared among the shadowy trees.

"We'll never find Mr Redbreast now," said Jess, as they clambered to their feet.

"Wait!" said Lily, frowning. "Freezy said they used their magic to shrink Mr Redbreast. And I'm sure I've seen a tiny robin somewhere before ..."

Jess grinned. "I know where! Everyone follow us!"

CHAPTER FIVE

The Sky Sparkles

Jess led the way as the four friends
hurried through the forest, scrambling
over the heavy snowdrifts.

"Where are we going?" called Isla,
puffing and panting in her magic snow
boots.

"You'll soon see!" said Jess.

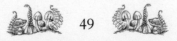

The falling snowflakes had become
a blizzard by the time they reached
Hollyberry Glade. Jess and Lily waded
through deep snow, examining the
decorations hanging from the tall fir trees.
"I'm sure it was here somewhere," Jess
murmured.

"There!" shouted Lily. She pointed
at the snowglobe they had seen earlier,
dangling from a branch, with a tiny robin
fluttering inside.

Goldie unhooked the snowglobe from
the tree and peered into it. "Goodness,
you're right!" she gasped. "It's Mr

Redbreast! Those mean snowmen must have shrunk him and stuck him inside."

The little robin flapped and fluttered as Jess took the snowglobe from Goldie. She unscrewed the base, and Mr Redbreast hopped out on to the snow. At once, the little bird began to grow, magically swelling until he was the size of a normal robin again.

 51

"What a relief!" exclaimed Mr Redbreast, flying up to perch on Goldie's shoulder. "Thank you so much – you've saved me! That naughty Freezy did this, and his horrible friends Blizzard and Buttons trapped me in the globe."

His beak chattered with cold.

"Poor Mr Redbreast," said Lily. "Let's get you warmed up."

"I saw some blankets in the cottage," said Isla.

"Good thinking!" said Jess.

Goldie carried the little bird back to his cottage in the tree trunk, and the

girls found some blankets in a tiny chest in the living room. They bundled up Mr Redbreast and set him down beside the blazing fire.

"Everything is such a mess!" said the robin, looking sadly round his little home. "Why did those snowmen do it?"

"They're helping Grizelda," said Isla. "She's cast a spell to steal the snow and ice from Snowdrop Slopes and bring it all over to Friendship Forest."

"We must stop her!" said Mr Redbreast. He hopped up and began to search through the books scattered on the floor. He pulled out a big leather-bound book with his beak, and flicked through it until he found what he was looking for.

"Here we are," he said. He pointed his beak at a drawing of white slopes, with magical lights dancing in a night sky.

"What are those?" wondered Jess.

"Why, those are the Sky Sparkles!" said Mr Redbreast. "They appear every night when dusk falls on Snowdrop Slopes. But they only shine for a little while."

"He's right," added Isla Waddlewing. "Sometimes my parents let me stay up late to watch them. They're so beautiful!"

"They certainly are," agreed Mr Redbreast. "They're powerful, too! If you can capture the Sky Sparkles and bury them in deep snow, you will be able to undo Grizelda's evil magic."

The girls felt a thrill of excitement. "Thank you, Mr Redbreast," Lily said. "Now that we know how to save Snowdrop Slopes and Friendship Forest too, we'd better hurry ... before all the animals have to leave for good!"

Story Two
Snowdrop Slopes

CHAPTER ONE

Family Sparklehoof to the Rescue!

The wind howled through the trees, and the snow fell so thick and fast that Lily could see nothing but a white haze beyond Mr Redbreast's little glade.

"This weather is terrible!" said Goldie, pulling her scarf up to her whiskers. "How

are we ever going to get to Snowdrop
Slopes?"

"I know!" said Jess. "What about the
Sparklehoof reindeer?"

Lily grinned. The girls had met the
flying reindeer during another adventure
in Friendship Forest. If anyone could
travel through the blizzard, it would be
them.

"Good idea!" said Mr Redbreast,
beaming. "We just need to call them to
us."

The little robin hopped over to a shelf
and took down some tiny golden bells.

"Ring these," he said, passing them to Goldie, Isla and the girls. "Wherever they are, the Sparklehoof family will hear."

Goldie shook hers first, and it rang with a sweet, soft chime. Isla joined in, then the girls. Each bell sounded with a different note, but together they made a beautiful ringing chime that seemed to echo through the forest.

"Look!" shouted Isla, pointing her little wing eagerly at the sky.

Lily glanced up and saw a shadow appear through the falling snow. It swooped down into the clearing, and Lily saw that it was all three of the Sparklehoof reindeers, pulling their red sleigh behind them. The reindeer trotted to a halt in the middle of the glade.

"Hello again, girls!" said Mistletoe, the biggest of the three. "We had a feeling it might be you calling for us. How can we help?"

"It's Grizelda," said Lily. "She's cast a

spell to bring all the ice and snow from Snowdrop Slopes to Friendship Forest."

"Oh, no!" the reindeer cried together.

"If we don't stop her, all the animals will have to leave," said Jess. "Will you take us to Snowdrop Slopes?"

"Of course!" chorused the reindeer. "Climb on board."

The girls scrambled into the beautiful red sleigh and sat on the wooden benches inside. Goldie and Isla sat opposite them.

"Ready!" called Lily.

The reindeer began to run, pulling the sleigh through the snow. Then all at once

they
leapt into
the air. Lily and
Jess held hands as they soared
upwards. Lily's hair flew back in the
icy wind, and she couldn't help grinning.
They were really flying in a magical
sleigh!

"Hold on

tight, girls,"

said Goldie, as they

flew up above the treetops. Jess

leaned over the side and saw the whole

forest laid out below, the trees dusted

with snow. "Oh dear," she said, pointing.

"There's Toadstool Glade ... but it's almost

completely buried."

The little animals were struggling to

wade through snowdrifts that reached up

to their chests.

"We have to find the Sky Sparkles in time," Lily said firmly.

"Look!" said Isla. "Snowdrop Slopes, up ahead!"

The girls saw that beyond the forest the ground rose and fell in soft snowy waves, with fir trees and cosy little cabins dotted here and there. But something was wrong.

The girls watched in astonishment as snow drifted up from the white slopes, carried by the wind towards Friendship Forest. In places, they could see little patches of green grass, where the snow had disappeared entirely from the slopes.

"It's snowing backwards!" said Lily.

The Sparklehoof reindeer began to swoop lower, and Jess realised that she wasn't cold any more. "It's warmer on Snowdrop Slopes than it was in Friendship Forest," she murmured.

Poor little Isla Waddlewing hung her beak, as though she were too sad to say a thing.

"It's worse than I thought,"

said Goldie gravely. "We've got only a few hours before sunset, when the Sky Sparkles will appear."

"Will we get to them in time?" asked Lily.

"I hope so," said Goldie. "If not, everyone will have to leave Friendship Forest and Snowdrop Slopes!"

CHAPTER TWO

Snow Shack

"We need to go that way!" called Isla, pointing to a little wooden chalet. It was nestled against a steep, icy slope and surrounded by snowy fir trees.

The Sparklehoof reindeer flew lower and lower until they landed next to the chalet, bringing the sleigh down with a

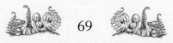

soft thump on the snow. Goldie, Isla and the girls hopped out.

"Thank you, Family Sparklehoof!" called Jess, waving as the reindeer took off again, pulling their magical sleigh after them. In a moment they were hidden by a spinning swirl of snowflakes, then they were gone.

Lily peered at the wooden chalet.
Icicles hung from the roof, but they
were dripping, melting in the warmth.
A brightly painted sign hung above the
door. It said "WADDLEWING SNOW
SHACK".

"Is this where you live?" Lily asked Isla.

Isla smiled and nodded. She looked
much happier now that she was home.
"My family make magical Snow Boots,
just like mine," she said proudly. "Come
on, girls, I'll show you!" She tapped her
boots and said,

"*Glittering ice,*

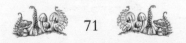

Skating is nice!"

Her boots glowed blue, and with a *ZZZAP!* and a shimmer of magic they transformed into ice skates again. Isla swung open the little wooden door and ducked through, followed by Goldie and the girls.

Jess shivered as they stepped inside. It was absolutely freezing! Her foot slipped on something and she wobbled. Then she saw why, and gasped. The whole floor was made of smooth ice.

"It's like an ice rink!" said Lily. Even the walls and the ceiling glittered with ice.

A door opened on the far side of the room, and five penguins skated in. "Isla!" shouted the biggest of them. "Thank goodness!"

Isla darted across the ice and met the other penguins in a big group hug. Then she turned to the girls. "This is Mum and Dad, and my brothers Shaun, Scotty and Todd."

The three little penguin brothers did a twirl and bowed, one after the other. Lily and Jess couldn't help giggling at the sight. "Pleased to meet you," they said politely.

"Pleased to meet you, too," said Mrs Waddlewing, but she looked anxious.

"Are you all right, Mrs Waddlewing?" asked Jess.

"Oh yes, dear, it's just that everything is melting so fast, I'm afraid that we might have to cancel the Ice Show."

"We might have to leave Snowdrop Slopes altogether," said Mr Waddlewing.

Isla's brothers hung their heads. "Even our lovely icy floor is melting!" said Todd.

"Don't worry," said Isla, giving her mum a hug. "We're going to catch some Sky Sparkles and bury them in the snow. Mr Redbreast says that'll break the spell!"

"What a clever robin!" said Mr Waddlewing. "But you'll need special pots for catching Sky Sparkles."

"Do you have any?" asked Goldie.

Mr Waddlewing shook his head. "I'm afraid not ... You need to go to the Wrinkletusks. They're a lovely family of walruses. They use Sky Sparkles to light up their home at night."

"They live just down the hill, by the sea," added Mrs Waddlewing. "They love splashing about in the water. Wait a moment, girls ..." She disappeared through the little door and returned with three pairs of magical Snow Boots. "Here," she said, handing a pair each to Lily, Jess and Goldie. "You can ski all the way there."

"Wow, thank you!" said Jess. "But we've never actually skied before."

"Don't worry," Isla told them. "The Snow Boots are magical! They won't let you fall."

Goldie, Isla and the girls said goodbye
to the Waddlewing family and stepped
out of the chalet. After the freezing ice
rink, it felt even warmer outside. But there
was still enough snow on the ground for
skiing. Isla led them all to the top of a
smooth slope, then tapped her boots and
said,

"*Slopes, bright and still,*
Let's ski down the hill!"

 77

ZZZAP! The boots glowed icy blue once again, and transformed into long, gleaming blue skis.

Goldie and the girls repeated the poem together. ZZZZZZZAP! Their boots turned into skis as well.

"Incredible," breathed Jess, in awe.

"It looks like a long way down," said Lily nervously. But there was no time to be scared.

"Ready?" said Isla. "One ... two ... three ... GO!"

CHAPTER THREE

Naughty Snowmen!

Isla shot down the slope, snow whooshing from beneath her skis.

"Here goes!" said Jess. She launched herself after the little penguin. Goldie followed, then Lily. At first she wobbled, but she soon got her balance. Faster and faster they went, until they were racing downhill, with fern trees blurring past on both sides.

"Wheeee!" said Jess. "This is amazing!"

"What was that?" gasped Goldie.

The girls looked just in time to see a bolt of icy blue magic whizz past and strike a fir tree. There was a creaking sound, and the fir tree began to shrink, until it was no bigger than a pot plant.

"The snowmen must be here!" said Lily.

Sure enough, Freezy, Blizzard and Buttons came sliding out from behind a tree, waving their stick arms angrily.

"Follow me," called Isla, swerving away

from the snowmen.

The girls and Goldie followed the little penguin as she darted in among the trees, steering nimbly between the trunks with big sweeps of her skis.

"There's a ramp up ahead," said Jess. She pointed to where the snowy ground rose up steeply, in a glittering icy slope.

"It's a ski jump," Isla explained. "We'll leap right over the canyon and land safely on the other side. Best of all, the snowmen won't be able to follow us, because they don't have any skis!"

"Great idea, Isla!" said Lily, trying to

sound brave even though she was nervous.

"Crouch down low," said Isla, "and you'll go faster. I'll kick up some snow to slow the snowmen down!"

The girls and Goldie whizzed towards the jump, while Isla skied in big circles behind them, throwing up snow like clouds of dust. Jess reached out and took hold of Lily's hand, and together they shot up the jump and launched into the air.

As they soared higher and higher, Lily couldn't resist a quick glance down. Her heart pounded as she saw the steep sides of the canyon far below. Jess closed her

 eyes,
trying
not to think
about how far it
was to the snowy ground.

Then the next moment they
were falling again, until – *THUMP!* –
they landed safely on the other side.

"Wow!" gasped Jess, as they slowed
down. "I want to do that again!"

The girls glanced back and saw Goldie
flying down from the sky after them,

her scarf trailing behind her. She landed
beside the girls.

"Where's Isla?" asked Lily.

Jess peered across the canyon and saw
that the snowmen had run out from
behind the trees. They were throwing

snowballs
at the poor
penguin,
forcing her to
zigzag from
side to side.
"Oh no," said
Jess. "It looks

like she's in trouble ..."

"Go, Isla!" shouted Goldie, as the little penguin dodged the snowballs.

Isla put on a burst of speed and raced up the ski jump, flying through the air. Halfway over the canyon she flipped into a somersault, before landing smartly beside them with a spray of snow.

Lily clapped. "Bravo!" she said.

"Thank you!" said Isla, beaming. "It's one of my tricks for the Ice Show!" Her face fell. "Oh, I do hope we can save the show ..."

"We're one step closer," said Goldie,

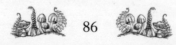

pointing down a short slope. "Look –
that's the Wrinkletusk family's igloo."

Lily and Jess saw a sparkling blue sea
stretching out from the bottom of the
slope, dotted with white icebergs. On the
icy shore a little round igloo stood, and
beside it were several roly-poly, furry
brown creatures.

"Walruses!" Lily said. "Come on!"

They all skied down the slope towards the igloo.

"Hello!" Isla called out, as they reached the icy shore.

"Well, if it isn't little Isla Waddlewing," said Mrs Wrinkletusk. She clapped her flippers together. "With all this nasty weather, it's a relief to see a friendly face!"

"This is Mr and Mrs Wrinkletusk," said Isla. "And Grandpa Wrinkletusk, and—"

"Don't forget me!" squeaked the littlest walrus. She rose up on her back flippers, showing sparkling white tusks. "My name is Maya Wrinkletusk."

"It's wonderful to meet you," said Jess. "But is everything all right? Why aren't you swimming in the sea?"

"It's too warm," said Grandpa Wrinkletusk gravely. He was the wrinkliest of them all. "Even our lovely icy home has started to melt. Soon we'll have to find a new place to live."

The girls saw that a puddle of water was spreading out around the igloo.

"We'll save your home," said Goldie.

"We just need to catch some Sky Sparkles!" said Jess. "Can we borrow some

of your special pots, please?"

"Of course!" said Mr Wrinkletusk. He lolloped into the igloo, and returned a moment later with a little stack of pots. Each one was made out of glittering, coloured ice, making the stack look like a little rainbow.

"They're beautiful," sighed Isla.

"Thank you!" piped up Maya. "We make them ourselves! The ice comes from a magical cave in the Rainbow Cliff. That's why it's so colourful."

"We'll make sure we return them safely," said Lily.

But just then a loud *SMASH!* made them all jump, and the purple pot Jess was holding exploded into a shower of icy shards.

"A snowball hit it!" Lily cried.

"Look!" gasped Goldie. "It's those naughty snowmen again!"

Lily's heart sank as she saw the three snowmen sliding down the snowy slope towards them. "They must have found a way around the canyon," she said.

"Quick," said Goldie. "Let's hide the pots, before they break them ..."

But it was too late. The snowmen let fly with a barrage of snowballs. *CRASH! SMASH! BASH!* Every last pot exploded in a rainbow of icy shards.

"They're all gone!" said Isla, her big eyes wide and her fluffy feathers bristling with shock. "What will we catch the Sky Sparkles in now?"

CHAPTER FOUR

Magical Icicles

"Ha ha!" shouted Blizzard, bouncing up and down on the spot. "Take that, smelly animals!"

"Now you'll never be able to undo the spell!" jeered Buttons.

"Let's tell Grizelda," sneered Freezy.

The three snowmen cackled and

 93

disappeared behind some trees.

"They're right," said Isla, hanging her head. "Soon all the snow will be gone from Snowdrop Slopes."

"We're not beaten yet," rumbled Grandpa Wrinkletusk. "You'll just have to make a new pot for the Sky Sparkles."

"And quickly," added Mr Wrinkletusk. "It'll be dusk soon, and the Sky Sparkles don't shine for long."

Outside the sky had already turned a deep blue.

"How do we make a new pot?" Jess asked the family of walruses.

Mrs Wrinkletusk pointed a flipper towards a cliff-face nearby. It shimmered red, blue, green and yellow, and at the bottom was a gaping, dark cavern. "First you need to collect some icicles from the cave in the Rainbow Cliff. And make sure you get all of the different colours!"

Maya passed a wicker basket to Lily. "You can use this," she said.

"Thank you," Lily said gratefully. "We won't let you down!"

The Wrinkletusk family waved their flippers as the girls, Isla and Goldie set out again, hurrying across the snow as fast as they could.

"These skis aren't so useful on flat ground, are they?" said Goldie, puffing and panting to keep up.

Lily looked down and saw that the snow was becoming hard and icy as they got closer to the Rainbow Cliff. "What if we change our Snow Boots into ice skates?" she suggested.

"Good idea!" said Isla.

"Skating!" said everyone together, and with four *ZZZAP*s and four shimmers of blue light, they were all wearing ice skates instead of skis.

They sped onwards, gliding over the icy
ground until they reached the Rainbow
Cliff.

Isla led the way into the cave and the
girls and Goldie gasped. The cavern was
entirely made of ice, with hundreds of
slender icicles dangling from the ceiling,
each one a different colour. Some glowed
white, whilst others were silver, pink,

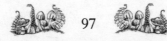

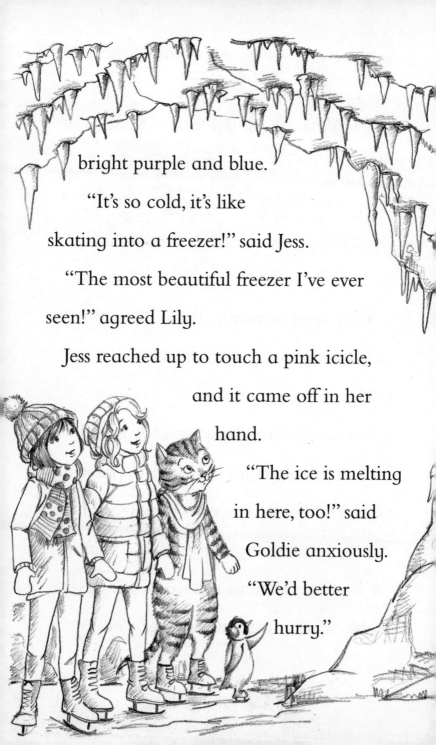

bright purple and blue.

"It's so cold, it's like
skating into a freezer!" said Jess.

"The most beautiful freezer I've ever
seen!" agreed Lily.

Jess reached up to touch a pink icicle,
and it came off in her
hand.

"The ice is melting
in here, too!" said
Goldie anxiously.
"We'd better
hurry."

They skated around the cavern,
cracking off icicles and piling them into

Maya's basket. Isla was the fastest,
whizzing round the cave, even skating
backwards and doing little twirls.

Soon the basket was full of glowing
coloured icicles.

"Now we just need to get back to the
igloo and make a new pot," said Lily.

But as they turned to leave the cave,
the girls saw three figures standing there
in the entrance, blocking out the light.

"It's those snowmen again!" groaned
Goldie. "Why won't they leave us alone?"

"Because you pests won't give up!"
shouted Buttons.

Before the girls could do anything,
Freezy and Blizzard lunged forward and
snatched Goldie with their stick arms. She
struggled, but they held her tightly.

"Don't be afraid, kitty," smirked
Buttons. "We're only going to put you in
a pretty snowglobe ..."

He raised his twiggy hand, and a ball
of icy magic began to swirl around it.

"Oh no!" cried Jess, covering her face
with her hands. "He's going to shrink
Goldie and trap her!"

CHAPTER FIVE

A Rainbow of Ice

"You leave my friend alone!" shouted Isla Waddlewing.

The little penguin dived on to her stomach and slid across the icy ground.

Whhhhsshh!

The ball of icy magic shot from Buttons's hand towards Goldie …

But just as it was about to hit, Isla
bumped into Goldie and the pair of them
went tumbling over and over. The bolt
of magic whooshed overhead and struck
the wall of the cave with an almighty
BANG!

The whole cave shook and icicles fell
from the ceiling, shattering on the ground

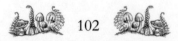

with musical chimes.

"Look out!" Jess called to the snowmen.
"If you're not careful the whole roof will
fall down."

Blizzard squealed as a pink icicle
smashed on to the ice right beside him.
"Let's get out of here, before those nasty
spiky things hurt us!"

The three snowmen turned and raced
out of the cave.

Goldie, Isla and the girls hurried out of
the cave too and skated back towards the
shore. The sun was red and low in the sky
now, and long shadows stretched across

the ice. It wouldn't be long until nightfall.

They were all out of breath by the time they got back to the igloo. The Wrinkletusks were waiting for them, crowded around Grandpa Wrinkletusk, who sat with a small stone basin in front of him. "Well done!" he said happily. "Now, put all the icicles in the basin."

Lily emptied the basket into the stone basin. At once the icicles fizzed and dissolved into a thick, swirling liquid – a rainbow of pink, purple, silver, blue and white.

"Perfect!" said Grandpa Wrinkletusk,

picking up a funny-looking object from beside the basin. It looked like a long pipe, made of stone.

"What's that?" asked Jess.

"You'll see," said Grandpa Wrinkletusk with a smile.

The old walrus pushed the pipe into
the swirling liquid, and sucked on the
other end – *WHSSSSHHH!* – until all the
liquid had rushed into the pipe.

For a moment the girls thought that
Grandpa Wrinkletusk was about to
swallow the liquid. But instead he raised
the pipe into the air and blew through it.
A bubble began to grow from the end of
the pipe, getting bigger every moment, the
colours shimmering across its surface.

"It's like an upside-down pot!" said Jess.

"That's exactly what it is!" said Maya
Wrinkletusk. She reached out and pulled

the pot off the top of the pipe. At once

the swirling colours froze into a beautiful

pattern. Maya passed the new pot to her

grandpa, who set it down on the snow.

"That's incredible!" said Isla. "It looks even more magical than the ones those mean snowmen smashed."

"I have to say, I'm rather proud of this one," said Grandpa Wrinkletusk, beaming. "Now, hurry, girls. You must take that pot to the highest point in Snowdrop Slopes if you're to have a chance of catching some Sky Sparkles!"

"Where's the highest point?" said Lily, picking up the pot.

"Sparkle Peak!" said Isla. "And I know the way ... Let's go!"

Story Three
Ice Show!

CHAPTER ONE

The Chillyhops' Chairlift

"Come on! Fast as you can!" called Isla, as she whizzed ahead on her skis. Isla, Goldie and the girls were racing across gentle snowy slopes, heading away from the little igloo and the glittering sea.

"How will we get up to Sparkle Peak?"

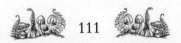

Jess asked the little penguin.

"I'm not sure," Isla admitted. "It's so high, even our magical Snow Boots won't be able to help us!"

Suddenly Goldie hit a bump and stumbled on her skis.

"Are you all right?" asked Jess.

"Yes, thank you," said Goldie, brushing down her fur. "But it's hard skiing uphill

... and it's even harder with all the snow disappearing!"

Goldie was right. Snow kept flying up into the air, thick and fast. There were patches of green grass everywhere, and they had to swerve from side to side to stay on the snow that was left.

"It's getting warmer, too," said Lily, unbuttoning her coat. "We'd better hurry, or Snowdrop Slopes will be in real trouble! The Wrinkletusks' little igloo will melt completely."

"And Mum and Dad's beautiful icy floor will disappear," said Isla sadly.

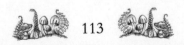

"And with all this snow flying over to Friendship Forest," added Jess, "the animals there will freeze. Grizelda's plan is working!"

"Not if we can catch those Sky Sparkles," said Goldie. "Oh, look!"

Up ahead, two peaks rose into the darkening sky, both coated in snow, with a curved valley in between them.

"If you tilt your head to one side, it looks like a lovely crescent moon," said Lily.

"Do you see the peak on the left?" said Isla, pointing to the taller of the two.

"That's where
we're heading.
Sparkle Peak!"

Jess groaned.

"But it's so far away! How will
we get to the top in time for sunset?"

Staring at a dark line that ran up the
side of Sparkle Peak, Lily said, "Is that a
chairlift?"

Little carriages dangled from the line,
and at the bottom of it was a wooden
cabin.

"It is!" said Goldie. "That's just what we

need. We can take it all the way up."

Feeling hopeful, they skied on, going even faster than before. At last they reached the bottom of the mountain, where the cabin stood. The door swung open, and three white arctic hares hopped out to meet them.

"Hi there!" said the biggest of the hares. "I'm Mr Chillyhop! This is my wife, Mrs Chillyhop, and our daughter, Freda."

The littlest hare hid behind her mother.

"She's a bit shy, I'm afraid," Mrs Chillyhop explained. "But what can we do for you? We run the chairlift up to Sparkle Peak. Everyone loves to go up and admire the view!" Her long white ears drooped. "Not today, though. We don't understand what's happening to all the snow!"

"Don't worry," said Jess. "We've come to put a stop to it. But to do that we need to get to the top of Sparkle Peak, so we can catch the Sky Sparkles."

"Goodness!" said Mr Chillyhop. "That's

very brave of you. Well, if it will help fix this terrible weather ... All aboard the chairlift!"

He led them to a shiny little yellow carriage that hung from the wire Lily had seen stretching all the way up the mountainside. There were two rows of seats in the carriage. Lily and Isla sat in the front, and Jess and Goldie in the back.

"Good luck, all of you!" called Mrs Chillyhop, as she pulled a big yellow lever beside the cabin.

At once the little carriage lurched upwards, sliding along the wire.

"Thank you!" Isla called back to the
Chillyhops. "I just hope we make it in
time ..."

As the little penguin spoke, the sun
dipped below the horizon. The snowy
mountainside gleamed orange as the
carriage whirred along its wire, climbing

 119

higher and higher.

"Look, you can see all of Snowdrop Slopes!" said Goldie, peering out the window. "Except there's hardly any snow left ..."

They could see only a few patches of white clinging to the slopes. Tufts of green grass poked up in patches, and there were no animals anywhere. The girls' hearts sank at the thought that Snowdrop Slopes might be abandoned entirely.

"At least Sparkle Peak has still got plenty of snow on it," said Jess. "For now

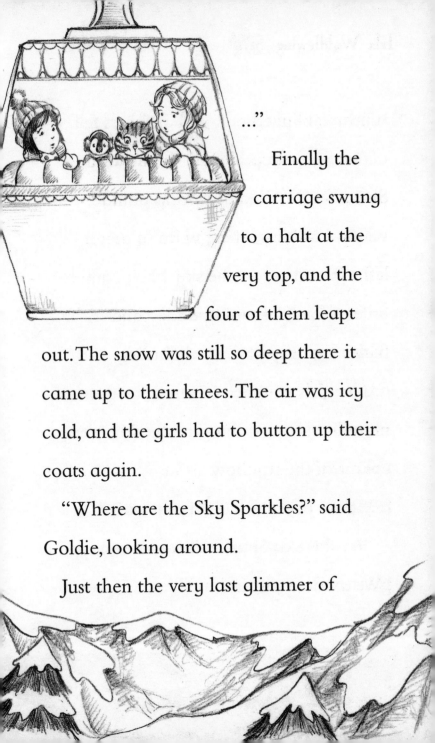

..."

Finally the carriage swung to a halt at the very top, and the four of them leapt out. The snow was still so deep there it came up to their knees. The air was icy cold, and the girls had to button up their coats again.

"Where are the Sky Sparkles?" said Goldie, looking around.

Just then the very last glimmer of

sunshine blinked out, and darkness fell across Snowdrop Slopes. There was a distant crackle like fireworks going off, and a shimmering wave of green light spread across the sky. Next came an explosion of pink sparkles, and a flickering of yellow like lightning.

The girls watched in amazement as more lights arced through the sky, every colour of the rainbow.

"It's so beautiful!" Lily murmured.

"It's the Sky Sparkles!" said Isla happily. "We made it just in time!"

CHAPTER TWO

The Biggest Jump Ever

"Let's catch some Sky Sparkles!" said Jess.

Lily took out the magical pot and swiped it through the air. But when she looked inside, there was nothing there.

"The Sky Sparkles are too high up!" said Goldie. "Try standing on tiptoes."

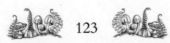

Isla Waddlewing

Jess took the pot and stretched up as high as she could. But she couldn't reach.

"Maybe we could stand on each other's shoulders?" said Isla.

Jess gave Isla the pot. Goldie hoisted the little penguin on to her shoulders. Then Jess and Lily picked up both of them. But Isla still couldn't reach the Sky Sparkles, even when she stood up and jumped off, as high as she could.

"It's no good," said Lily, as Isla landed in the snow. Lily and Jess put Goldie down next to Isla.

"How can we catch the Sky Sparkles if we can't reach them?" wondered Goldie.

"You can't!" said a sneering voice.

The girls whirled round and saw that Grizelda's three snowmen had arrived. The snowmen bent down and began to make snowballs.

"Give up, silly girls!" yelled Blizzard. He threw a snowball at them.

Lily dodged. "Hey, that's mean!"

The snowmen just cackled and kept
on pelting them with snowballs. The
four friends ducked behind the yellow
carriage and began to make snowballs
of their own. Lily and Jess leaned around
the carriage to throw them
at the snowmen. One
splattered on
Blizzard, and
another on
Buttons, but
the snowmen
just cackled.

"You can't stop us!" crowed Freezy.

"No ski jumps to escape here!" added Buttons.

"That's it!" cried Jess suddenly. "We can use a ski jump to get really high up in the air and reach the Sky Sparkles!"

"But where will we find a ski jump?" asked Goldie.

"I know!" said Isla. "Leave this to me."

The little penguin tapped her Snow Boots.

"*Soft snow, dark sky,*

It's time for me to snowboard high!"

ZZZAP! At once the boots sparkled and shimmered, transforming into a long blue snowboard.

"Wish me luck!" said Isla. She pointed to the valley below, which curved up to the smaller mountain peak, just like a ramp. "I'm going to snowboard down Sparkle Peak and up the other mountain," she said breathlessly. "If I go fast enough I can do a really big jump off the top of it

... the biggest jump ever!"

"That's brilliant!" said Lily. "We'll keep those nasty snowmen busy."

Isla crouched down low on her snowboard, holding the pot ready. She did a little hop, and then she was away, speeding out from behind the shiny carriage, whizzing past the snowmen and down the side of Sparkle Peak.

The girls leaned round the side of the carriage to watch. They saw Isla get smaller and smaller, until she was just a little black dot whooshing down the mountain into the valley.

"Look how fast she's going!" said Jess.

"She's going to jump!" shouted Goldie,
as Isla shot up the second peak.

The little penguin flew up into the sky,
somersaulting towards the Sky Sparkles ...
then came tumbling down again, her little
wings flapping hopelessly.

"Oh no!" gasped Goldie. "She's missed!"

CHAPTER THREE

A Lovely Snowy Home

Isla raced down into the valley again, then back to the top of Sparkle Peak. She slid to a halt beside her friends. "The Sky Sparkles are so high up!" she said sadly. "I don't think I'm good enough to reach them by snowboarding."

"If you can't do it, no one can! You're

the fastest skater in Snowdrop Slopes,

remember?" Lily told her.

"And the best skier," said Goldie.

"And jumper!" added Jess.

Isla proudly puffed out her chest.

"Do you really think so? Well, in

that case ..."

The little penguin kicked off

again. She raced down into the

valley and up the slope of the

smaller mountain. But this

time, when she reached

the top, she turned round and came back
again, throwing up huge sprays of snow
as she climbed higher and higher
towards her friends ...

"I think she's going to jump off
Sparkle Peak!" said Lily.

"Go, Isla!" shouted
Goldie.

WHOOOSH!

Isla flew
past

the carriage and
up into the air.

"Nooo!"
shouted the
snowmen.

But there was
nothing they
could do. Isla

reached up high, scooping Sky Sparkles
into her pot, one coloured light after
another. She did a neat somersault, and
landed next to the girls with a soft *flumph*
of snow. Her little pot shone brightly with
the Sky Sparkles trapped inside it.

"You did it!" shouted Jess.

"Hurray!" cried Lily and Goldie.

"Thank you," said Isla bashfully. "I couldn't have done it without you all!"

The Sky Sparkles started to fade a little in the sky. The colours weren't as bright and then, with a fizzling noise, they disappeared, leaving only the soft white glow of the moon.

"Just in time!" said Goldie.

"Oh no, you're not!" shouted Buttons. The girls turned and saw that the snowmen had appeared.

"We're going to smash your pot to

135

smithereens," sneered Blizzard, scooping up snow to make another snowball.

"Protect the pot!" cried Lily.

The girls, Goldie and Isla huddled round, forming a wall in front of the pot. Then Isla began to dig with her wings.

"Hurry!" said Goldie. "We need to bury the Sky Sparkles to undo Grizelda's spell."

"Take that!" yelled Freezy, and he lobbed a snowball as hard as he could.

Wump! The snowball hit Lily's back. But she could barely feel it.

"It's turned to water straight away!" said Jess. "The snow's melting so quickly, even the snowballs can't last."

Buttons threw a snowball next, but it melted halfway through the air.

"If we can't break your pot, we'll shrink you all!" shouted Blizzard. He stuck out his stick arm, but he only managed a little fizzle of blue light.

Lily put her hands on her hips and

turned to face the snowmen. "You know, you're being very silly!" she said sternly. "What do you think will happen when the snow melts?"

Buttons scratched his head with a twiggy hand. "We've never really thought about it," he said. His carrot nose fell off, and he leaned down to stick it back on.

"You're all going to melt!" said Jess. "Don't you see? If Snowdrop Slopes keep

getting warmer, it's not just the animals who'll have to leave ... You won't be able to stay either!"

"That would be terrible!" said Freezy sadly. "It's so nice here."

"It certainly is," said Goldie. "So how do you think the poor animals will feel if their homes are ruined?"

The snowmen hung their heads.

"You're right," said Buttons. "We have been silly. Grizelda told us we'd have a lovely snowy home in Friendship Forest if we helped her."

"There's already a lovely snowy home

139

for you," said Isla. "Here, in Snowdrop
Slopes. It's winter all year round! And
there are lots of nice animals here who
love the snow, just like you do."

"That sounds wonderful," said Buttons.

"Well then, you're very welcome to
stay," Isla said.

"But first, we need to save Snowdrop
Slopes and Friendship Forest," said Jess,
"Do you promise to stop helping Grizelda
and causing trouble?"

The snowmen all looked at each other
and then nodded.

"We promise," said Blizzard. "We want

to be friends with all of you instead."

"Brilliant!" said Goldie. "But there's no
time to lose. We have to bury the pot of
Sky Sparkles before the snow disappears.
We can do it if we work together."

Goldie, Isla and the girls knelt down
in the snow and started digging. In a
few moments, they had made a big hole,
ready for the pot. Isla placed it carefully

at the bottom, then Lily and Goldie
pushed all the snow back into the hole,
and Jess patted it down until it was flat.

They stood up and looked around.
Jess's heart sank when she saw that there
was just a tiny sprinkling of snow left
on the tops of the two peaks. The rest of
the mountainside had turned green and
brown, with not a speck of white left on
it.

"Did it work?" said Isla nervously.

"I don't know," whispered Goldie.
"Maybe we're too late!"

CHAPTER FOUR

The Star of the Show

The friends waited and waited, but
nothing happened.

"I can't believe it," said Isla. Her eyes
filled with tears. "This is the end of
Snowdrop Slopes!"

Lily and Jess each took one of the little
penguin's wings in their hands to comfort

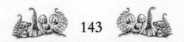

her. Goldie joined paws with them, forming a circle.

"We've ruined everything!" said Freezy sadly.

"We're so sorry," said Blizzard. His carrot nose drooped, and Buttons had to push it back in.

"Wait!" gasped Lily. "Do you see that?"

Something had come whooshing out of the snow, just where they had buried the pot of Sky Sparkles. It was a big, shimmering surge of light, so bright they all had to shield their eyes. It shot through the sky in a perfect arc.

"It looks like a rainbow," said Jess.

"But the colours are different!" added Goldie.

The rainbow had stripes of pearly white, icy blue, pale sunrise pink, sparkling silver and sunset purple. It ended at the top of the next peak, twinkling in the night sky.

"It's not a rainbow," said Isla, her big eyes open wide. "It's a snowbow!"

In the bright glow of the snowbow, Lily could see all the way to Friendship Forest. In the distance, above the trees, a white haze rose up and rushed towards them.

"The snow is coming back!" she cried. "It worked after all!"

Soon they all felt snowflakes falling in a glittering white flurry.

"Hooray!" shouted the snowmen. "You saved Snowdrop Slopes!" They began to bounce up and down, waving their twig arms happily as the snow fell thicker and faster all around.

Just then, a train whistle blew somewhere far below. *TOOT!*

"That sounds like the Friendship Forest Express!" said Goldie. "It must have come all the way from the forest."

Isla clapped her wings together in delight. "Everyone has come for the Ice Show! Will you girls come and watch it too?"

Jess and Lily grinned at each other. "Of course we will!" they said together.

Lily, Jess and Goldie sat on big, soft blue cushions at the side of a glittering ice

rink. Animals sat all around the rink,
wrapped up in blankets, woolly hats and
scarves, talking excitedly to each other.

It was still snowing, but seeing the
animals so happy made the girls feel
warm inside. They had saved Snowdrop
Slopes and Friendship Forest, and
Lily and Jess smiled at the sight of the
snowbow twinkling overhead, casting a
magical light over the ice rink and all the
animals.

"You did it, girls!" said a familiar voice.

They turned to see Mr Redbreast the
robin hopping over to them. He wore

a thick woolly scarf and his chest was neatly groomed.

"Hello, Mr Redbreast!" said Jess. "Wow, you're looking so much better now!"

"Fit as a fiddle," said Mr Redbreast. "All thanks to you! You've saved us all, you know."

"We'd do anything for Friendship Forest," said Lily. "But we couldn't have done it without you."

"Happy to help," said Mr Redbreast. "Where's our little friend Isla? I should thank her too!"

"You'll see," said Goldie, with a smile.

Just then, a small brass band began to
play a cheery tune, and all the animals
hushed. The girls' stomachs fizzed with
excitement. The Ice Show was about to
begin!

Lily and Jess watched in amazement
as the animals of Snowdrop Slopes
performed, one after another. The
Chillyhop family began with an
incredible dance in the snow. The

Wrinkletusks demonstrated some magical
ice blowing to gasps and applause.
There was skiing, snowboarding and
tobogganing down the slopes.

Then the brass band stopped playing,
and all the animals went very quiet, as
the star of the show stepped out on to the
ice.

"It's Isla!" whispered Jess.

The little penguin wore a sparkly blue
waistcoat. She didn't look nervous at
all as she took a bow. Then she was off,
skating around the rink.

Lily gasped. Isla was an even more

amazing ice-skater than she had thought! She spun, jumped and twirled. She did backwards somersaults and pirouettes. All the animals seemed to be holding their breath in astonishment. Then at last Isla leapt into the air for a final twirl and landed on one skate, fluffy wings outstretched.

The crowd erupted into applause.

"Go, Isla!" shouted Jess, clapping as hard as she could.

"Whoooop!" called Goldie.

Isla had the biggest grin the girls had ever seen. She straightened her waistcoat and bowed low.

Then Lily gasped in shock. "Jess," she murmured. "Do you see what I see?"

Jess gazed up at the snowbow and spotted an orb of sickly green light come swishing out from behind it. It whizzed closer and closer until it hovered in mid-air above the ice rink.

"Oh no," cried Jess. "It's Grizelda!"

CHAPTER FIVE

Just Like Buttons

CRACK!

The ball of green light exploded in a shower of smelly sparks. Grizelda came flying out of it and landed on the snow beside the ice rink. The animals sitting nearby jumped up and scurried away, hiding behind snowdrifts and peering out

 155

anxiously at the nasty witch.

Grizelda scowled at the Enchanted Snowmen. "What do you think you're doing? Watching this pathetic little show, are you? You're useless!"

Her gaze fell on Lily and Jess, and her green hair twitched with fury. "You rotten girls wrecked everything!" she roared. "But it's not over. I've got lots more plans to take over Friendship Forest and drive out these smelly animals."

"You leave them alone!" shouted Buttons.

"We're not helping you any more!"

yelled Freezy crossly.

"We're going to live here in Snowdrop Slopes with our new friends!" added Blizzard.

The snowmen began making snowballs and pelting Grizelda with them.

"Stop that or I'll turn you back into the silly snowballs you started out as!" snapped the witch, as a snowball whizzed past her ear. "Yowch!" she cried, as another hit her tummy. She tried to dodge, but her boot slipped on a patch of ice and she went flying, landing on her bottom. *Flumph!*

The animals all began to giggle.

"It's not funny!" screeched Grizelda.

She lurched to her feet and slipped again,
landing face down in the snow. "Curses!"
she growled as she sat up. Snow dripped
from the end of her hooked nose. "You
haven't seen the last of me! Just you wait!"

The witch threw her cloak around her.

Then with another deafening *CRACK* she disappeared, leaving nothing behind her but a puff of green smoke and smelly sparks.

"Hurrah!" cheered the animals. "The snowmen saved us!" They hoisted Freezy, Blizzard and Buttons up into the air and carried them around the ice rink in triumph.

Lily and Jess grinned at each other.

"It'll be dark again soon," said Goldie, pointing up at the snowbow. Its light was fading away, leaving just the black sky dotted with little white stars. "Time for us all to be going."

"We'll give you a ride in our sleigh," said the three Sparklehoof reindeer, trotting over to the girls.

"Thank you," said Jess.

But as she and Lily stood up, a little fluffy cannonball shot towards them and wrapped them up in a big hug. "I'm going to miss you," said Isla, holding on to them tightly.

"We'll miss you too!" said Lily, laughing. "But we'll be back to visit, we promise."

"Thank you, girls," said Freezy. Jess

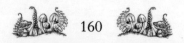

looked up and
saw that the
animals had put
the snowmen
down at last.

"We'll be good
from now on,"
said Blizzard.

"I'm going to live with the Waddlewings.
Mr Waddlewing says I can help him build
snow jumps for the animals to practise
on!"

"And I'm going to live with the
Chillyhops," said Freezy. "I'll help them

shrink snowdrifts so the animals can get up to Sparkle Peak safely."

"What about you, Buttons?" asked Jess.

"The Wrinkletusks said I can live with them," said Buttons. "I'll help them make pots and decorations out of icicles. Actually, I've already made something. Look!" He held out a shiny little blue disc.

"It's a button!" said Lily.

Buttons nodded. "I made it out of a blue icicle from the Rainbow Cliff cave. I want you girls to have it! It's a little gift from us snowmen, to say sorry."

"Thank you!" said Jess.

"And we forgive you, of course," added Lily. When they had finished saying their goodbyes, the girls and Goldie climbed into the Sparklehoofs' sleigh, and the reindeer took off, flying through the darkness until they had left Snowdrop Slopes far behind.

At last they flew down among the trees of Friendship Forest, and landed in a moonlit Toadstool Glade. The girls jumped out, relieved to feel grass beneath their feet. "The snow is all gone!" said Lily.

"Everything's back to normal," said Jess,

with a happy sigh.

"Thanks to you girls," said Goldie. "And there's the Friendship Tree."

"Will we see you again soon?" asked Jess.

"I'm sure you will," said Goldie.

"And if Grizelda tries anything, please come and fetch us," said Lily, "We always want to help."

"I will, thank you," Goldie promised, smiling at them both.

The girls hugged their cat friend. Then with a final wave, they opened the door in the trunk of the Friendship Tree.

Golden light spilled from inside, and they stepped through ...

A moment later the girls stood in Brightley Meadow again. Everything was just as it had been when they left – white and peaceful, with the snow falling gently all around. Hand in hand, they ran back across the stream and into the garden. Their snowman was still standing there, waiting for them.

"We never gave him his nose!" said Jess.

"I've got just the thing," said Lily with a grin. She reached into her pocket and brought out the shiny blue button. Then she pushed it into the snowman's face and stood back. "Finished!"

"Aww," said Jess. She grinned back at Lily. "He looks just like Buttons!"

The End

Jess and Lily are heading to the enchanted Spelltop School! Can they stop Grizelda from spoiling the magic?

Turn over for a sneak peek of the next adventure,

Charlotte Waggytail
Learns a Lesson

"These pups are so adorable!" exclaimed Jess Forester. She and her best friend, Lily Hart, were in Lily's back garden. The autumn sunshine was warm on their backs. They were sitting in a wooden pen, playing with three tiny, golden puppies with flappy ears and curly tails.

"Someone handed them in to Helping Paw this morning," said Lily.

Lily's parents were vets, and they ran the Helping Paw Wildlife Hospital from a converted barn at the bottom of their garden. Lily and Jess spent every minute they could caring for the animal patients.

Jess scooped up the smallest puppy and giggled as it nibbled her blonde hair. It felt warm and soft in her arms. "They're unusual," she said. "What breed are they?"

"I'm not sure." Lily opened a book that lay at her feet. "I asked Mum and Dad, but they don't know either, so I got this book about dog breeds from the library."

Jess put her pup gently on the grass and bent over the book. "These puppies have squashy black noses like pugs but their ears are floppier." The pup pulled at her trainer laces. "Hey, don't do that, you cheeky thing!" Lily said with a giggle.

Jess picked up a rubber bone. "Play with this instead."

She rolled the bone across the pen. To her surprise, a paw poked out from under a blanket and batted the toy back.

A cat with gleaming golden fur crawled out from the blanket. She stretched and gave a friendly miaow.

"Goldie!" cried Lily.

"She's come to take us to Friendship Forest!" said Jess, beaming.

Friendship Forest was a magical land where the animals lived in wonderful woodland houses – and best of all, they

could talk! Lily and Jess loved to go to
their secret world with Goldie.

Goldie sprang out of the pen. Lily and
Jess stepped out after her and shut the
dogs safely inside.

"We'll be back before you know it,"
said Lily, blowing the puppies a kiss. No
time passed in the human world while the
girls were visiting Friendship Forest.

Goldie scampered out of the garden
and across the stepping stones of
Brightley Stream.

They followed her to the old, dead-
looking tree in the middle of Brightley

Meadow. As she got near, the tree sprang into life. Every branch shimmered with red, gold and brown leaves. Shiny green acorns popped up and squirrels chased around the trunk. Sweet singing filled the air as greenfinches swooped and dived in the dappled sunbeams.

Goldie touched the trunk with her paw and writing appeared on the bark. Giving each other an excited smile, Lily and Jess held hands and read the words aloud.

"Friendship Forest!"

A door appeared in the trunk. Jess turned the handle. As the door opened, a warm yellow light flooded out. They tingled as they stepped through, which they knew meant they were shrinking, just a little. Then the warm light faded and they were in a clearing of blossom-covered trees that smelled of strawberries and cream.

Goldie was now standing on her back legs and wearing a glittery scarf around her neck. She was nearly as tall as the girls' shoulders, and they hardly had to bend to give her a happy hug.

"I'm so glad you could come," she told them. "Today's the first day of term at

Spelltop School. Would you like to help the new little pupils settle in?"

"Yes please!" cried Lily, her dark hair swishing in excitement.

"We've never seen the school before!" said Jess, delighted.

Goldie led them through the forest, down a path lined with periwinkles and cheerful primroses.

Read

Charlotte Waggytail
Learns a Lesson

to find out what happens next!

Magic
Animal Friends

Look out for the brand-new
Magic Animal Friends series!

Series Seven

There's lots of fun for everyone at www.magicanimalfriends.com

Play games and explore the secret world of Friendship Forest, where animals can talk!

Join the Magic Animal Friends Club!

⭐ Special competitions ⭐
⭐ Exclusive content ⭐
⭐ All the latest Magic Animal Friends news! ⭐

To join the Club, simply go to

www.magicanimalfriends.com/join-our-club/